A New Home on the Prairie

by Kerri Anne Wray
illustrated by Alan Flinn

Harcourt
SCHOOL PUBLISHERS

Printed in China

ISBN 10: 0-15-350783-7
ISBN 13: 978-0-15-350783-0

Ordering Options
ISBN 10: 0-15-350601-6 (Grade 4 On-Level Collection)
ISBN 13: 978-0-15-350601-7 (Grade 4 On-Level Collection)
ISBN 10: 0-15-357920-X (package of 5)
ISBN 13: 978-0-15-357920-2 (package of 5)

4 5 6 7 8 9 10 0940 12 11 10 09

"Well, children, this is it—our new home,"
Pa said, pointing to a wide field and forest.
Tim, Emily, and Beth looked out the back of
the covered wagon and saw nothing but tall
weeds and trees.

"I don't see anything, Pa. Where is it?"
asked Beth, looking around.

"Why, it's right here! You see, in time, we'll
have a cabin and a barn and a field of crops,"
Pa said with a smile. Tim, Emily, and Beth
looked at each other confused. Where were
the other houses? What about the stores and
streets? How could they possibly live here?

Ma, Pa, Uncle Jonas, and the children got down from the wagon and walked around. It was May, and there was a gentle breeze blowing across the prairie. The tall weeds shook in the wind, and the trees in the nearby grove swayed back and forth. The adults knew that turning this section of land into a home would require a lot of hard work. They also knew that it would be worth it.

"Jonas, I can see it all in my mind," Pa exclaimed, looking around. "The cabin can go here, the barn over there, and farther back, we can plant the corn."

Ma and Pa and the children had lived in Philadelphia, but Pa had had a hard time making a living there as a printer. When he and Ma heard about free land in Missouri, they decided to take a chance and move. Uncle Jonas was Pa's brother, and he, too, wanted to make a new life.

They sold many of their belongings, bought a covered wagon, and made the long, dangerous journey. It was an extremely rough ride for Tim, who was eleven, Emily, who was nine, and Beth, who was five.

"Now the first thing we need to do is build a shelter. We're going to stay in the shelter until we get our log cabin built," Pa explained. Then he and Uncle Jonas took axes from the wagon and walked off toward the woods to gather some tree branches and logs.

"Come, children, we're going to pull up some of these weeds so there's a placc for the shelter," said Ma.

"When are we going to eat lunch?" asked Tim.

"We need to be responsible and get some chores done first," Ma answered firmly.

The family slept in the wagon while the shelter was being built. Pa and Uncle Jonas used logs and branches to make a structure that had three walls and a roof. It was not a very strong shelter. So Pa warned the children not to jostle it, or it might fall down.

On the third night, the family prepared to sleep in the shelter for the first time. They placed their blankets on the ground and got in. It was not very comfortable.

"I don't like it here," Emily said quietly to Beth.

"I want to go back to Philadelphia," replied Beth sadly.

For the next six weeks, Pa and Uncle Jonas worked on building the log cabin. Tim helped Pa as much as possible, while Ma and the girls prepared the meals and worked the land.

At sundown, the mosquitoes came out in full force, and the children tried their best to keep the bugs off of them. "I'm getting bit again!" exclaimed Emily, scratching her arms.

"Come sit by the fire. The smoke keeps the bugs away," replied Pa.

"We never got bit up like this back home," Tim muttered to Emily.

Finally, the cabin was built, and the family moved into it. The children were still unhappy with their new home, however.

"Ma, can we please move back to Philadelphia?" Tim asked one day. "We don't like it here."

"Oh, Tim, this is your home now. It's the place where you're going to live until you're an adult," said Ma kindly.

"I miss my friends and my house," he said. Ma was attentive and listened to Tim. Then she gave him a big hug and told him that he would get used to it here soon, but Tim just wandered away sadly.

One day in mid-July, Ma and the children were standing in front of the cabin talking about the chores that needed to get done. Just then, a rabbit darted out of the tall weeds nearby, chased by a red fox. Both Beth and Emily ran straight into Ma's arms. The rabbit swerved to avoid the fox, but a moment later the fox pounced on the rabbit and dragged it away.

"That's why I tell you to always watch out for wild animals," Ma said.

"I want to go back into the cabin," declared Beth. She ran off, and Emily quickly followed.

That afternoon the skies darkened, and the
wind picked up. "A storm is coming," said Pa
to Ma. Ma walked out to the field where the
children were picking weeds.

"Children, come back to the cabin now.
A storm is coming," she said. Just as they
reached the front door, a loud clap of thunder
boomed in the sky, and there was a flash of
lightning. Pa and Uncle Jonas closed the door
tightly as heavy rain poured down from
the sky.

The children huddled in the corner with Ma, as frightened as they had ever been. Pa and Uncle Jonas looked at the ceiling of the cabin, hoping it would not collapse.

The wind kept blowing, and some of the mud caked between the logs of the cabin blew off. Rain came into the cabin and got the floor wet. The thunder and lightning continued, too. Ma did her best to comfort the children. Finally, after an hour, the storm passed.

A few days later, the children were still unhappy. Ma said to Pa, "We have to *somehow* help these children accept their new life here."

The next morning, Pa and Ma took the kids out to the field. "Now look out there," Pa said, pointing to the open prairie. "What are some things you can do out there?"

"There is nothing to do here," replied Tim.

"You say that because you're used to Philadelphia," Pa said. "However, there are all kinds of things you can do out here! You can catch bugs and fish and frogs! You can climb trees! You say there is *nothing* to do, but actually there is *everything* to do! It's a contradiction, but it's true: this place has nothing *and* everything!"

13

Then Ma said, "From now on, we want you to have fun here, because this is a truly special place to live." The children looked at each other puzzled. They really hadn't thought about things quite that way before.

"Emily, let's go look for some frogs," declared Tim with a smile. The children ran off. Ma and Pa looked at each other and smiled. Now they knew everything was going to work out just right.

Think Critically

1. How did the children feel about their new home at the beginning of the story?

2. What did Pa and Ma say to help the children change their opinion of their new home?

3. Why did the family sleep in the covered wagon for a few days?

4. How was the family's home on the prairie different from their home in Philadelphia?

5. Does anyone in the story remind you of someone you know? Why?

 Social Studies

Find Out The family in this story moved to Missouri. Find out some things about Missouri, including what year Missouri became a state. Then list at least five more facts about Missouri.

School-Home Connection Share this story with a family member. Then have a discussion about what it would be like to live on the prairie in a log cabin. What would be the best part? The worst part?

Word Count: 1,157